Adjacent

Smiles

The Love We Make

The sun sleeps next to you and only rises when you open your eyes. How can I not smile at the joy of witnessing it every morning? And how could I hope to find more when you are so much more than what I ever dreamed? I pray you can share in the smile you brought to my life.

Lacresha N. Hayes

LANICO MEDIA HOUSE

Words that wield power, imagination and life

Arkansas•Texas•Louisiana

Cover Design © 2015 Jesse Kimmel-Freeman

ISBN: 978-0-9862057-4-3

Lanico Media House
Imprint Company of Lanico Enterprise
www.LanicoMediaHouse.com

Printed in the United States of America
First printing: April 2015
10 9 8 7 6 5 4 3 2 1

Other Books by the Author

The Rape of Innocence: Taking Captivity Captive

Becoming: My Personal Memoirs

Raw Redemption

Truth and Intimacy: A Couple's Journal

Poetic Infinity: Passion and Promise

A Heart in Motion

Heart Strings

Unnecessary Roughness

Cascade of Tears

Tangled

The Ultimate Survival Guide for the Entrepreneurial Woman

The Path to Oneness

Black Dakota

The Snare of a Strange Woman

For the man who doubted love, the lion who needed courage, and the king who needed a queen. I needed your inspiration!

Acknowledgments i
Introduction 1
The Seven Stages..2
    Stage 1: The Picturesque Scene 2
    Stage 2: Invoked Passions...2
    Stage 3: Whispers without Words......................................2
    Stage 4: A Collage of Dreams...3
    Stage 5: The Naked Truth..3
    Stage 6: The Connection..3
    Stage 7: The Testing...4
The Picturesque Scene...5
    If Not at First..7
Invoked Passions 10
Whispers Without Words..14
    Trip Wire 17
A Collage of Dreams 18
The Naked Truth 21
    Laid Bare..24
The Connection 27
The Testing 30
What is Happily Ever After: The Epilogue 33
Excerpts 36
About The Author 42

Acknowledgments

Facebook has given me the opportunity to make many great friends and business connections. I suppose I'm most grateful for my authors whose drive keep me inspired. I'd like to acknowledge all of my Lanico Media House authors, to encourage them to keep pushing as they have encouraged me to do so with my personal writing.

I'd like to further acknowledge Jesse Kimmel-Freeman, my partner in creative crime. I love you, girl!

Introduction

This book is something totally different from what I usually write, which is healing manuals and books that make you think and deal with hidden pain. Well this time, I tapped into my hopeful romantic side and I decided to tell a love story.

The story in this book is based upon some of the stuff I saw and even went through. I felt it needed to be shared because we are losing our faith in love by the droves. But romance and love are not dead. They live and in many relationships that are blooming, they are both thriving. The problem is we hear those crying from broken hearts because their tears are louder than the happy people's joy. They are telling their story of pain and frustration while the happy people are so busy being happy they hadn't bothered to sound the joyful alarm that relationships are wonderful.

I hope you enjoy this story as I narrate it. I hope you equally enjoy the insights I share throughout the story. For a moment, put away your doubt and clear your mind. Prepare for a beautiful journey. To happy reading!

The Seven Stages

In my opinion, relationships all seem to go through seven stages. If any relationship survives it all, I truly believe they last forever. This book is all about finding and securing happily ever after. It is imperative to identify your stages of relationship and to deal with it accordingly and maturely. So let me give you an overview of each chapter, the seven various stages of a relationship.

Stage 1: The Picturesque Scene

This is the meeting and point of interest. This is the beginning of whatever will transpire between the couple. Many people fantasize about a great one, but end up with a happenstance event providing their very own picturesque scene. You see, the discovery is that wherever love finds you first will always be a beautiful scene to remember.

Stage 2: Invoked Passions

Is it hot in here, or is it me? Yes, this is that stage. Your desires come alive. You want to know and be with this person. Goosebumps are common. Smiling, blushing, and daydreaming are all common signs. Maybe you aren't quite the romantic and for you, this stage looks like making a pros and con list about the potential mate across from you.

Stage 3: Whispers without Words

All that passion has cooled just enough for you to begin thinking about what you're doing. This stage is about questions and usually the place where doubt and fear can really rear its ugly head. But this is also the stage that can create the bond that will withstand the trials of life.

Stage 4: A Collage of Dreams

After the questions have been asked and answered, and matters of reserve have been handled, the dreams step in. This is the stage where the couple begins to think of each other in future terms: buying houses, having babies, getting a joint bank account, getting married, etc. This is also the stage when the doting love of stage 2 has quieted enough for the desire for one another to grow deeper than physical, when skills and strengths are considered and factored in.

Stage 5: The Naked Truth

At this stage, the relationship moves into the harsher truths. These truths are when couples begin to realize the other party isn't perfect and their life is not instantly and always perfect with them. They have to deal with both the real strengths and real weaknesses of the other party and also their own. Some relationships do not make it beyond stage five because some people discover their relationship was based upon a superficial bond. Also, the truth of our personal, relationship maturity is tested here because for the serial daters, they simply cannot accept the fact that no one is perfect. But for those who are mature, who have found what they need in one another, this stage will be the cord that binds.

Stage 6: The Connection

After the couple goes through the stages above, a genuine connection forms. This isn't as much about time as it is about honest intimacy. The connection for some couples will not be enough to build a lifelong relationship, but that's perfectly okay.

Stage 7: The Testing

There are some who view the word test as something negative, when all it really does is measure your level of understanding in a particular area. In relationships, tests only gauge various aspects of it. It isn't bad. It is necessary and when you realize it is an assessment tool that can help you improve your own life, then you learn to appreciate tests, to take them honestly, and to work on problem areas revealed by them. After the testing comes the reward and it is worth it!

The Picturesque Scene

It's cold outside

And the trees are bare

The skies are dull

And as blank as a stare

But when you stepped out the door

I swear I saw the sun

Suddenly the middle of winter

Felt like spring had begun

Then you smiled at me

The temperature rose a few degrees

When you opened your mouth

Out came a summer breeze

I was taken right away

And there was no shame

Nothing to extinguish me

My heart was aflame

Where did this dashing prince come from when you weren't looking? Isn't it funny how love almost always blindsides you? I mean, you're sitting there swearing off dating, love, and finally settling into your life as a single man or woman. You hadn't shaved in weeks. No special grooming. No attention-getting perfume or cologne. You are clearly not looking for love. And then, BAM, out of nowhere, it seems your heart gets snatched away!

Were you on errand to get a loaf of bread from the grocery store? Maybe you were in a long line at the post office or barbershop? Wherever you were when you were seized by love, it was a picturesque scene, not because of the actual location, but because of the miracle of connection. Let me tell you a little story.

I knew a young lady who grew up with pretty much the same white picket fence dreams as others in her generation. She always thought love would be tall, dark, handsome, chivalrous, and brave. Though her life was tough, the little ember of hope that love would find her never died. It shifted in importance and thus as a source of major disappointment to minor irritation.

When she was young, she figured love would come early. As her twenties passed, she remained hopeful for her thirties. As they drew to a close, she had begun to think less and plan less to be a part of something special, of coupledom, but the hope still remained. And as spoken in 1 Corinthians, faith, hope and love abides. Her abiding hope was answered!

On a happenstance trip with a not-quite friend, she met the guy who would become her greatest love. You know, love is a funny thing and falling in love is as unique as the people who are falling. For some, it happens a lot like the movies, else the movies would probably not exist. For others, it happens in the strangest, most random of ways. For some, love happens in beautiful parks, scenic locations, mansions, premiers, and trips to exotic beaches. But in this instance, it happened in a trailer park. Oh wait! Don't laugh. Let me set the scene.

A dirt drive full of potholes. An old trailer. As she and her friend pulled up to the scene, she didn't expect to find love there. In fact, she wasn't even sure she'd find friendship or even mutual respect. She had no expectations. She simply hoped to find a few jokes and a good wi-fi signal as promised. But you gotta love the irony of finding what you are no longer seeking after wearing yourself out looking for it previously. I mean, how often have you torn the room apart looking for the remote, your keys, or some other item that seems to have disappeared into thin air? If you're like me, you probably didn't find them in the heat of your seeking. It was after some kind of rest that what you wanted manifested itself again. Well, that was the case here.

He met them at the door, and I won't insult anyone by saying it wasn't love or even like at first sight. It was just a man who met two women at his door. He spoke and he joked and he interacted with his company, but there was no strikes of lightning or spiritual quickening. There was only the sound of a person being human. Still she had no clue that the voice she was hearing would become her favorite sound. She didn't know the eyes she had only glimpsed would become her favorite pastime. There was nothing discernible in that first happenstance meeting. But he was paying closer attention than she was and the sun was about to break forth in her life! A miracle was brewing!

If Not at First...

So while my friend didn't recognize her love right away, he did recognize her on some basic level. And so wouldn't you know it, not a whole 24 hours went by before he initiated further contact? Now, you'd think maybe my friend, the intellectual that she can be at times, would have tuned in at that point, but she didn't. The years of frustration made her a tad slow on her feet. After a Facebook message or two, she found herself looking at his profile. She pondered a friendship. I mean, a nice respectful man as a friend is an asset. She viewed a picture or two. She read a couple of posts. But lightning still didn't strike. There was no quickening, no goosebumps, and no thundering epiphany.

A few days and more messages went by. She allowed curiosity to take her to his page again and then again. Maybe, just maybe, they could be friends. He wanted to see her, but she just could not look at his pictures and get inspired to see anything more than someone she could occasionally hang out with when she was in the area.

The not-quite friend seemed to be around more often and my friend found herself asking about her potential new friend. Everything sounded lovely, but she was still quite slow to even consider that this happenstance man might be the right man for her.

Finally, she decided after a few more days and messages to see him again. She'd go alone just to see if maybe he'd be fun to hang out with even without their mutual association. After all, her not-quite friend spoke highly of him and even considered him to be her best friend. She didn't put anything extra into her appearance that first evening, namely because she had no romantic intentions. Though he'd hinted at it via Facebook, she wasn't convinced.

They sat and talked in his bedroom. He didn't say anything spectacular, nothing memorable for her. But there was something else that she did notice: how comfortable she was in his presence alone, how respectful he was of her natural attractiveness, and how his eyes actually reminded her of a waterfall with the sun beaming overhead. Still though, she didn't dare even entertain the idea of love. Attraction, yes! Love, no. But then her visit ended.

As he walked her to her car, careful to keep a safe distance, she had a thought: should she hug him or no? She pondered a second too long and decided to do something different. She decided to hug him. And then the lightning still didn't strike, but something different did. A flood of calm and clarity swept through her, though at the moment it happened, she had no words for it. There seemed to come a knowing that brought a perfect peace with it. No, she didn't know who exactly he was to be yet, but she knew he was certainly sent for her for some blessed purpose. He belonged in her life, though how long and for what exact purpose, she still didn't know.

Here I want to interject a little bit about the man and his feelings. People don't think men get excited about love, about the prospect of it, the building of it, and the longevity of it, but they do. He looks across a room and sees something. It could be the shape of her eyes when she smiles or the glow of her skin. But he sees something that intrigues. He hears her voice and his heart takes flight. He wonders about her and finds himself driven to know her. But when a man has been hurt and disappointed, sometimes he quietens his process, but he cannot stop it. This wonderful guy, a controlled assassin, chess player, strategic thinker, knew there was something perfectly right about my friend, even though she hadn't tried to leave that impression or any impression really. Oh, I think if we could know the process of real and lasting love from both parties simultaneously, we'd experience a rash of couples working it out and sticking it out for the sake of the moment that began it all because that moment is worth more than anything else couples will build or buy together in a lifetime. Ahh, the moment.

So, before my friend could make it home 20 minutes away, he sent a text just to say he enjoyed the visit and wanted her to come back again as soon as she could. Ha, I get conflicted here because there was an adjacent smile shared between them in that moment, though they were not in the same location to experience it visually. So I want to tell his story, but I need to tell hers. Anyway, here is what I can say about them both. In the realm of energy, theirs had aligned to be open to one another. He wanted her and she was, for a moment, very glad and honored to be wanted by him. A light was seen in the distance though she had no clue how large the light actually was, but at least she had been made aware of light. What a scene they had painted free from sinful, lust, lies or expectations--- they had colored the atmosphere with hope. Absolutely divine!

Invoked Passions

There are a thousand parts

That compose my love

And I want to kiss them all

There are a million places

And a million ways

I hear love's call

When he comes home

I sit at his feet

There is no other place I'd rather be

When he has a need

I rush to assist

This is love everyone can see

I serve and attend

I listen to understand

We come together to form a plan

I never imagined

I could love this way

God must have sent this man

You've probably never really looked passion up in the dictionary. I've spoken to a lot of people and that is one of the words most of us never feel the need to define. I think that could be because it is different for us all. Or it could be because we believe passion is something to experience rather than define. I challenge you to write your personal definition of the word, and then to look it up in your dictionary and write out the definition below your personal definition. You may be pleasantly surprised to find that the dictionary falls short of what you feel when you set yourself to define it personally.

In the days after that magical night which wouldn't appear very magical to the regular onlooker, my friend chatted with and even found herself looking forward to a message from her new friend. Hope was mounting inside her faster than flood waters in a Category 5 storm! He wanted to see her for Valentine's Day. But the reality was, she was in a relationship already. A Valentine's Day rendezvous was nearly impossible. And now, she wasn't so sure she wanted to see him again because anything after that initial solo meeting would be like cheating. She was no cheater. Still, he pressed and everything inside her wanted to make him happy. So without thinking, she agreed to at least drop by on Love day. How telling was that! I mean, had she literally just decided his order of importance in her life? She'd put someone above her boyfriend of nearly four years. She had passed over family, lifelong friends, and business associations for her boyfriend. But here she was about to open up a space for her new friend that could jeopardize her already-sinking relationship.

You know, passion is a noun. More directly, it is an experience. It is a drive. An urge that burns through every thought thrown at it. Well, my friend had had her passions awakened over the course of days. She couldn't explain the need to keep revisiting his page, his photos, and his various writings. She couldn't explain her desire to know him beyond what words could describe. She was flowing on pure spontaneity and energy, not stopping long enough to add expectations and fear. She was being pulled by something and it felt more amazing by the minute!

On Valentine's Day she made room for him in her day. Later she'd figure out she'd given him space in more than her day, but in her heart also. She visited with him, this time paying attention to the atmosphere, looking more closely at this man she couldn't stop thinking about. But didn't dare cross the line that would cause her to become a cheater or heartbreaker. They talked, joked, were interrupted by another one of his friends, and still managed to have a great time, albeit short. He didn't want her to leave. Neither did she want to leave, but she was duty bound to spend that evening and night with someone else. A moment of sadness seized her at that thought, but she shoved it aside and continued on with her life as planned before her pleasant distraction.

On her drive home, she replayed every word he'd said. She tried to hear it as he said it, tried to ferret out what heart his words were born in. She was all smiles but with a major obstacle, a relationship with another man. When she did arrive home, her boyfriend was not there. In fact, she found him elsewhere, inebriated, and being very disrespectful. Dysfunction is hard to stomach, but it becomes exponentially more difficult once you've been treated well, have experienced some peace, or hoped again for dignity and respect. An argument transpired and what would have normally been answered by simply leaving for a few hours quickly became a fight of major proportions and marked the end of that relationship.

There are times when people are added to our lives for their strengths because we need to borrow what we simply have had robbed from us. I think this new guy's kindness and energy captured my friend. I think her conversations with him were infusing her with courage and strength. And in the right time, an opportunity opened for her to walk out of what she had long outgrown. Her passions had been invoked and there was no way she could go back to her dull, lackluster life she tolerated because she feared what might lie outside of the walls of her relationship prison.

As she headed to her sister's house to gain perspective, her sister passed her in traffic headed to the Valentine's party she was supposed to attend also. She followed her newfound adventurousness and called her new friend who quickly invited her back. And in a night of weakness, she and he nearly completely ruined their chances at lasting love by moving right into a relationship. They didn't give her time to heal, the breakup pain time to ebb away, or him time to be sure. But love always finds a way, even past bad decisions and fear. Yes, love conquers all!

Whispers Without Words

Umm, this is good

Coming together with you

Yes I am a little afraid

But that tells me this is true

Umm, you touch me

Ooh, it feels so good

But I want to make sure

I love you like I should

I've been hurt before

And, ooo, the pain

It took the life out of me

I cried tears like rain

Hmm, you wouldn't hurt me, huh

You wouldn't play a game

Nah, I know better

Love is always above blame

Even children can read body language and I think most of us are fairly proficient at it by adulthood. We can generally discern anger, sadness, or sickness without needing to be told. We think we know love when we see it, hear it, or feel it. We have all these words and feelings but often struggle to use them simultaneously. But in some ways, this is the most beautiful aspect of falling in love. It is not the words that are said, but the whispers from the heart that has no words to interpret them. It is in those whispers that real relationship is created, defined, fortified, and maintained.

Not everyone is in tune with themselves which causes them to make decisions that are contrary to their true nature. Being in tune with yourself will help you make better decisions for your life, and especially when it concerns matters of the heart. Knowing what matters to you most helps you keep your priorities firmly in sight, and helps you protect them from frivolous decision-making. Believe it or not, one frivolous decision can bring years of torment. This is particularly so in relationships. A bond formed too soon, on shaky ground, or with the wrong person can hinder you possibly for the rest of your life. It can be that serious. That's why we must learn to relate on deeper levels than just physical attraction. The presence of attraction does not mean a relationship is expedient. A relationship should be made by way of a conscious decision rather than as a reaction to feelings and urges.

People are quite unique, beautiful, and delicate. Just because we're used to seeing harsh treatment of the human soul does not mean that is appropriate. The beauty of love is that it brings back the sensitivity, especially in the beginning. It's like a fresh awakening and suddenly you're hearing birds chirp, feeling the coolness of the dew, and watching the sunsets of life. In the beginning, when it is real, it is as if two people tune into each other's frequency and begin picking up spiritual, physical, and emotional cues. In fact, dare I say the majority of what we learn from others, particularly our mate, does not come from the words spoken? It comes from energy frequencies and other nonverbal cues.

As two hearts seek to meet and discover one another, there are screams. We all know about the screams. There are also whispers, some of them with words and some of them that have no words to define them. They are like groans, grunts, or sighs. And it is in this place of whispers without words that is so glorious and magnificent that I shudder to attempt to describe it, except that I was blessed to truly witness it and I know the story of love on a deeper level must be told.

My friend and her beau made love on Valentine's night, and in so many ways, married each other that night. He asked her to stay again and again, and by the third day, asked her to move in with him. He didn't want to be away from her even a moment. She didn't want to be away from him. They were like children who could not get enough of each other. But nothing in this life is perfect, which only adds to the wonder of how anything lasts in this world.

In that first week, my friend was invigorated by this new man in her life. Just thinking about him gave her energy and creativity. She cooked, cleaned, paid extra attention to her appearance, and went out of her way to honor him in every way she knew how. She pulled out the lingerie and props. She put aside her sexual fears, not really by force of will, but because she wanted to taste every inch of him, to smell every inch of him, to truly see it and experience his body in totality. Yes, she was in love! That is what love does, opens you up to see the beautiful mystery of the creation. She stared at him all the time, especially in his eyes which seemed to captivate her day after day. But the fact is, she had just left another man who she didn't want but still cared for. That was the first mistake, the first challenge and nearly the last.

My friend's new beau wasn't a man of many words. Fact is, he didn't need to talk much because she could feel his energy so clearly. When he did speak, she listened for what was said and for what wasn't. And when he slept at night, she could discern whispers that came from him, the sigh of "finally," and the groan of fear because he didn't want her to hurt him. He'd been hurt and disappointed a lot. He didn't know how to ask for special care, but he needed it and she knew it. So she set about to serve him as the king she saw. She refused to ask questions of the past because it truly didn't matter to her. He was royalty and he was her love. Being with him made her feel as if other men never really existed. But other men did exist and soon the love bubble would pop when the inaudible whispers of his heart collided with the ties she had to her past.

All of us have things inside us we cannot verbalize that burns in our heart and mind daily and continuously. I'm sure most people agree no one wants to be hurt in a relationship. But when you've been hurt before, you can become more fearful of love. It can be hard to trust. It can be hard to truly embrace someone. There are millions of people in half-assed relationships. They are in them, may even want them to work, but they are also reserved, suspicious, and maybe even to the point of self-sabotage. They are consumed with the fearful screams of past experience and the inaudible whispers of hope, that someone will truly love them, want them, seek them, protect them, and honor them perfectly. But there is no perfect in relationships… there is only the process of perfecting, as in life. So because this is the reality and reality isn't as attractive as the fantasy, many people quit before they ever begin, never give their relationships a chance, and float between people as they seek something that does not exist in a ready-made fashion. A relationship **must** be built! Simple as that.

Trip Wire

As their relationship proceeded, problems began to crop up as they learned more about each other. They were both quite stubborn and prone to wanting things their own way. But amazingly, I saw something new in my friend. She had finally learned to love enough not to insist upon her way. Sure, I witnessed more than a few temper tantrums, but at the end of the day, her joy made him happy. But as her ex continued to interfere with their relationship and his friends continued with the gossip and suppositions, his hidden fears were brought to the forefront. Her feistiness and stubbornness began to kick in. And for a short time, they divided and became like enemies. He didn't trust her and held himself in reserve. She rebelled against his withdrawal with tantrums and made mistakes that only made his fear greater. In fact, she nearly single-handedly destroyed all the magic that had brought them together, not because she was guilty of any infidelity, but because she lacked patience and temperance. She wanted it too fast and didn't understand why his love bubble was not working like hers was. She lost sight of the fact that sometimes it takes work to build trust. His fear had been triggered and there was nothing that could fix it but time and patient love.

A Collage of Dreams

He attempted to mold me

At first I rebelled

I wasn't having it

I threw fits and yelled

Then he showed me a picture

He wanted me in it

But I needed a trim

If I were to fit

We discussed the future

We shared our dreams

We nipped and tucked

We adjusted the seams

Compromise is beautiful

We chose to build together

We are constructing a home

That endures stormy weather

You have dreams. You have had them all your life. Maybe they aren't glamorous, but they are yet your dreams. As life happens, they may evolve and grow. In hardships, they may all but die. But they exist.

When a couple comes together, their dreams form a collage. It may not always look beautiful in the beginning, but that is the point of working together and growing together. They make it beautiful and make it work for something bigger than either of them were on their own. A collage of dreams.

Think about all the happy family photos you have ever seen. Think about the old couples you see who still love one another. Think about the children, grandchildren, and other family. Think about the home, the secrets that home holds of how each couple works out their coupledom. Doesn't it remind you of a tapestry? There are tragedies and joys that bind couples together in the face of differences and weaknesses.

My friend's beau was probably one of the best barbers she'd ever seen. He had a steady hand, creativity, and truly cared about each cut. He worked a state job also. He was one of those guys who had a lot of talents, including writing, and had yet to truly tap into his own greatness. He had dreams and was patient and calculating enough to bring them to fruition.

My friend was spontaneous, creative, and driven. She was the type you could come to with ideas and get results. Oddly, she wasn't necessarily a detail-oriented person, but she had the sure willpower to make herself sit down, learn, and manifest things. She was a tremendous business woman, multi-talented, but she did not possess patience as her beau did.

The two of them coming together was almost poetic. She could manifest must quicker than he could, but he could plan, calculate, and maintain in ways she never could. They were complete opposites, like fire and water. But where most people would see only the inability for the two to co-exist, they both chose to enjoy the power the other possessed. She could put him out. He could heat her up. It was a beautiful balance they had to strike, not one of ease either.

As days turned to weeks, several times they found themselves having to make room for each other's dreams. There were days when he had to remind her to get back to business, days when she had to understand he had to work on his craft rather than do the couple stuff she so longed for. Days when she had to go and represent her businesses. Days when he had a bad day at work and simply did not have the energy to be sweet and loving as he was when they first met. But they continued making the sacrifices. Yes, sacrifice is not easy to make, but love makes it easier. I watched as these two worked out their balance and believe me, the sight was not always pretty. In fact, several times, I didn't think they'd make it, but love always finds a way. It may not happen immediately, but it will happen.

The Naked Truth

The two hearts are afraid

Though they had it made

They counted their fears

While shedding unnecessary tears

The two minds are confused

Both terrified of being used

Their inner violence

Makes them choose silence

The two pair of hands release

Thinking to increase

But it only brought misery

Not at all how it should be

She breaks away

Though she wants to stay

He shoves her out

And listens to doubt

And in all of this, they did not truly pray

They tried to continue in the same way

But love intervened and reunited

Once they made sure God was invited

How do you define truth? Amazingly, everyone has their own definition of truth though it is not up for interpretation. Almost everything is fluid and changing. Almost. But not truth. For those of you who are thinking about changing facts, let's remember that facts are subject to change - as in the number of known planets - but truth is constant. So again, how do you define truth?

One truth that affects us all is the truth of love as an entity to itself. There is nothing else like it. There are no equivalents. Love is a creative force, empowering, and nurturing. Another truth that we must embrace is the truth of individual rights. Her desires and needs do not outweigh his or vice versa. They both are free to choose for themselves. The kicker is that after a relationship has been formed, the right is not revoked, but other considerations are added to it. She can choose for herself. He can choose for himself. But both decisions affect the other party and so require each person to lean heavily on the law and truth of love. Otherwise trespass is inevitable.

In this beautiful interaction between these lovely souls, truth was not relied upon as heavily as it needed to be, mainly because both parties had been scarred tremendously. Distrust made them keep the things they should have said and say the things that should have never been said. Watching them struggle to love each other properly was actually quite inspirational. Both wanted to pretend they didn't care but they did. Both wanted to pretend they were still in control, but they weren't. It was like watching children struggle to walk for the first time, an absolute joy to behold, even when it brought tears, yells, and sleepless nights.

I regret to tell you that my friend and her beau were broken up at the end of their first month together. Yet, they had squeezed years of loving into that little short month. But it was through the break up that truth would come galloping in. She'd realize that yes, she was indeed in love and not the kind she typically called love but real love she could not control. He'd realize that yes, she was completely irreplaceable and while she was a complex individual, she was also exactly what he needed. The naked truth was about to come crashing into their lives in each other's absence and that may not have ever happened without a period of separation.

Laid Bare

I think one of my favorite aspects of personal relationship with God is that there is absolutely nothing hidden from Him at any time. He is always in a place of knowing and understanding and never caught off guard by anything we do as humans. Now on the other hand, human knowledge is extremely limited. We only know what we have been taught or exposed to otherwise.

In a relationship, things would be much easier if couples could share their personal truths with each other in the same vein they are felt in. If we knew each other in complete nudity emotional and spiritually, there would be fewer misunderstandings, much more mercy, and more relationships would last, happily.

After countless arguments and misunderstandings, after distrust became their language, my friend left her love. She thought jumping up and storming out would end the relationship, and it did. But it did not end the attachment in her heart. She was still every bit as in love with him as she had been the days prior to their disagreements. On the other end, he was tired, worn down, suspicious, and hurting. He didn't understand her complexities, and frankly was already tired of trying. He felt relationships should be simpler, less painful. He'd been through quite a few things, but he was determined not to endure more heartache at her hands. So he let her go and began cutting every tie that would remind him of her. They made a solid decision to let it go, but she was not prepared for what came next.

I think it pretty much goes without saying that it takes time to heal a broken heart. There are times, however, when not even time heals the broken heart because more so than time, we must give our hearts resolution. You can leave a love and be gone for thirty years. But one day, if you never deal with what you felt and finalize it, when you see them again or have reason to remember them, you will be pulled and tugged and it will not end no matter how many pep talks you give yourself.

My friend walked out of the uncomfortable part of the relationship just to walk into the sure torture of being without the one you love. It further added pain to her to know he still loved her no matter how angry or bitter he was. After a couple of days, she began to realize her mistake but could not get back to that love bubble with her beau. He was hardened toward her, cold, and cruel. He wanted his heart to mend and thought cutting her off completely would heal him. But just as she could not forget about him, he could not forget about her. Still, with her lack of self-control and impulsiveness, she suffered through tons of mistakes and missteps in an attempt to deal with the increasing yearning she had for him. She had ended it, but it felt as if someone had ripped him away from her. Her pain was real, palpable and continuous. I ached for her as I watched her struggle to pick up the pieces of her heart without losing all of what she'd built.

On the other side of town, a man was broken inside. He was questioning if happiness was going to reside with him, if he'd ever have a love to call his own. He replayed it all, not always because he wanted to, but because she'd literally pierced his life in every area. He missed coming home to a clean, fresh home. He missed the meals. He missed the tenderness and care. He missed her smile. He missed her back massages, her gentle caresses, and the sure presence of her energy. He wasn't the only one either. His brother missed her and loved her. His friends and family noticed a change in him. And then there was Facebook. Even after unfriending her, she somehow ended up in his newsfeed, mainly because his brother was constantly liking stuff on her page. She was a superstar in the making, and in fact, becoming a household name via her businesses, books, and coaching. He just couldn't seem to make her fade away. She continued to call him from time to time, the occasional "I still love you" texts, and various questions she always had kept him vacillating between anger and pain. Why couldn't she just disappear? Why was her absence such a hole in his heart? He couldn't make his feelings leave immediately, but he knew that eventually, they would die. At least, he hoped they would.

In the following months, they both dated others, trying on new people like clothes in a boutique. She went through quite a few guys, hoping to find a spark with someone, but none existed. At the end of every day and the beginning of every morning, he was still in her heart. She couldn't really kiss anyone else because she only wanted his lips. She couldn't make love to anyone because she couldn't bear the thought of cheating on him. Yes, she still felt being intimate with someone else would be cheating on him because he was indeed her love, the man she'd been praying for all those years of going through emotional relationship drama. She knew it like she knew her name. His eyes were inside her even in his absence and she simply could not dismiss it or even hide it. More than once, in the presence of other men, she'd broken down at the thought of him. But she continued trying to date and staying active to attempt to get over him. After a couple of weeks, she gave up with the text messages and phone calls. It was clear he wanted no further contact. And after another few weeks, her tears were limited to romance movies, love songs, and late, sleepless nights when she swore she could hear his voice. The love simply would not die.

His dating attempts were not much different. He slept with a few women here and there, had a few sleepovers, but not one of the women ever looked at him the way my friend had. None of them adored him as much and he knew it. Even the ones who did special things for him did not dull the occasional ache of his loss. He had loved her and he knew that. He had high hopes for them. He saw power and love and potential in her. He missed her but no amount of alcohol, kicking it, or sex could fill the hole in his heart. He thought of calling and texting her several times, but he simply could not get over all the questions. Had she cheated on him? What did she want with him? Was she truly devious or had she truly been lied on? One part of him wanted to believe in her but he had seen women run game and he didn't want to be a victim again. So he steadied himself, stayed clear of her, and waited on his love for her to die.

Now to everyone else, it made no sense for them to be broken up when they cared so much for each other. But while in the relationship, they'd maintained cover to protect themselves from one another. Sometimes, it takes the continuous ache of loss to peel back the layers and masks that cover us up. Apart, these two were stripped down to their core, laid completely bare. And in times like that, either you accept what truly lies at the center of your heart and act on it, or you ignore it and continue on trying to dull the pain and pretend like it isn't there. Each person has to make their own choice.

The Connection

In that first touch

In the first hour

They were connected

The connection was power

In that first kiss

In the first hug

They were addicted

Their love was a drug

But the second time around

And the second connection

Was stronger than the first

Because God had given correction

The thing that joins them

The power of their love

Is not of this earth

It is from above

In most cases, for a connection to happen, there must be a point of touching and agreement. Most cases, but not all.

Because of the separation and the ache to see him every day, my friend finally left town. She couldn't handle how it felt to be so close but still so far away from him. As she began traveling again, promoting her business and books, the excitement of success helped her fight the urge to run back to him, but it was truly a moment by moment battle. No amount of money or success could replace him.

He remained where he'd always been. He continued his usual daily pattern. He finally adjusted to the idea of having to find someone else to love. He thought of her on various occasions, but it didn't hurt as bad as it had. In fact, from time to time, he found himself amused by some memory of her.

It had been a few months since they'd last seen each other. One night as he scrolled his Facebook timeline, he saw a picture of her. He didn't quite expect it, but his stomach got butterflies all over again. It was like he was seeing her again for the first time. It wasn't her best photo, but she was looking directly at the camera and it felt as if she was looking directly at him. And in that moment, he missed her as intensely as he did the first time she'd walked out. It felt like he was starting all over again with the grieving process. He couldn't help it. He clicked like on the picture, not sure what, if anything, that would start. He read a few of her posts and it appeared she was still single. He wasn't sure why that brought him a slight smile, but it did. He never wanted to share her with anyone. He was sure she'd been with someone, but she was apparently not connected to anyone exclusively.

My friend saw his like on her picture. And for all intents and purposes, her heart melted. Had he really just liked one of her pictures? She stared at the picture trying to figure out why he'd liked that one in particular. She tried to figure out if the like meant anything. But being the impulsive creature that she was, she immediately went to his page and browsed around. Nothing seemed out of place. So she sent him a short, sweet message, hoping she would not end up feeling rejected. It simply read:

Thanks for the like. It's nice to "hear" from you. You have been missed.

It had been long enough for her to gain her bearings about herself so she didn't sit and wait on a response. She said a little prayer and continued on with her postings and such. A few minutes later, however, she did get a reply. And as much as she tried to control it, her whole spirit was uplifted and she could not stop the huge smile that spread across her face. His response was:

And so have you. How are you?

After months of no contact, there they were having a normal conversation on Facebook. Yes, they had truly missed each other. And while they both were still a little apprehensive, they were both equally if not more so excited to be back in touch with one another.

Weeks went by with them speaking online on occasion. But every message made them feel reconnected. They hadn't seen each other, hadn't talked on the phone, and hadn't texted. But those Facebook messages had reawakened the love they both haphazardly chunked in the wind some four months earlier. However, it had been meant because their first try had been tarnished from the beginning. Truly, they were on the brink of a second chance, one they could make better than the first if they were smart, honest, and open. Some things cannot be rushed or fabricated and one of those things is love. A love connection must be nurtured in truth and must be given patience and acceptance.

My friend had hurt for him so long that the thought of a second chance made her cautious and prayerful. She couldn't bear losing him a second time. He had been through enough emotional turmoil behind their break up that he didn't want to rush things. He still had the questions but he wouldn't ask them. He wouldn't bring it up until he knew in his heart he could trust her answer. After all, it was a trust issue that had split them up the first time. But this time would be different, this connection deeper, the love surer.

The Testing

In a small cabin

I contemplate

Should I come back

Or is it too late

I pace the floor

I miss you so

I want to run

But have nowhere to go

In this cabin

Where we first kissed

I write you a love letter

Because you are missed

As I head to the door

I take one last glance

I'm not going to believe

This is our last chance

How many times have you heard the saying, "tried and true"? Probably a ton of them. Well, anything tried and true has been tested. Tests are a part of life as certain as taxes and death. Cars are tested. The material that goes into building your home is tested. Our medications are tested. Tests are required to prove the efficiency of things and the heart of people.

As my friend and her beau worked on reconnecting slowly and lovingly, there were several tests thrown their way. There was the test of patience. The test of respect. The test of time. The test of trust. But mainly, there was the test of love.

Both of them proceeded with caution they could barely maintain for the joy and excitement of having back the great aspects of their relationship. The times when they weren't messaging was not because they were not thinking of one another. It was them both exercising control and waiting on the relationship to reform naturally. It required a great deal of trust and patience to work their way through the lingering pain at how the relationship had ended the first time. He had to learn to trust her words and she had to learn to respect his right to disagree and his position to lead. They both had to give it time and they both had to practice having faith in each other. They were being tested.

After a couple of months, my friend was aching to see her beau. He wanted her to come visit also. Finally, she grabbed her courage and drove back to Arkansas, primarily to see him. The trip back home didn't seem so long as she replayed their first go around in her head. Within seven hours, she was pulling up at his place, that same place where she'd fell in love.

She paused a moment before getting out of the car. And just like the first time, he met her on the porch. When she saw him walk out the door, her heart completely melted. And like no time had passed, she loved him again as fiercely and true as she had in the beginning. A tear welled up but she smiled and swallowed it down.

When he saw her car pull up, he tried not to rush right out to meet her, but he did anyway. She still looked as beautiful and as loving as she ever did. Somehow, seeing her again quelled all the questions. All that remained was the longing to touch her, kiss her, and hold her. He couldn't remember why he'd let her go before but he was sure he wouldn't lose her again.

He didn't know how to proceed, as he often didn't. But she walked right into his arms with a hug that made it seem as if she'd always been there. She looked up at him and he knew for certain she was the one he loved. After all those months, he'd lost nothing. In fact, it felt as if he'd grown more in love with her.

In their first true embrace, one without lies or facades, or fears, the benefit of separation became apparent. Somehow, they'd learned to appreciate each other. They had decided they both deserved a chance. They were no longer afraid of being hurt by the other. They'd been there and done that. So, in the light of truth, nothing remained of the past but the love.

For every test they had been through, it all seemed worth it. Every tear during those long nights had fed and nurtured something that was destined for happily ever after. But it was not automatic. It was a choice!

What is Happily Ever After: The Epilogue

My friend and her beau, well now her husband, worked through their fears and issues. They decided to do what was necessary to make their relationship work and it paid off. They got their happily ever after. But then, what is happily ever after?

It isn't riding off into the sunset and living a blissfully unaware life for 20, 30 or 40 years. It would be nice if it was like a movie, but the happily ever after is nothing like the movies.

Actually, happily ever after looks more like a couple who gets married. Maybe they purchase a home eventually, or continue renting or leasing. Maybe they have children together or help each other support children they had already. But however they work it out, they still endure hardships, still go through pain and uncertainty, and still must continue to choose each other every single day.

In the happily ever after, there will be deaths in the family, maybe the loss of jobs and things. There will be struggles and fears that try to cripple the couple. But if they choose to remain together, not just in a physical aspect, but in every way on every level, then they will find that the true and sure blessedness of relationship is the companionship and support through the dark times, the love and hope shared each moment of the day. You see, happily ever after is a choice that is made each moment. Happily ever after only happens by choice. It cannot be forced or manipulated. It happens through the bond that couple has.

I have many favorites when it concerns movies and almost all of them are romantic in nature. What girl doesn't desire to have a man chase her down, convince her of his love, and then sweep her off her feet into a happy life? We all fantasize. But at this point in my life, I realize that real life is actually more beautiful than any movie ending.

Look at the old couple at the park. They have been together for 45 years. She still fusses over him and his clothes, wiping his mouth, driving him crazy. He still thinks the young men and old men envy him of his beautiful bride. He still watches her walk, though feeble, because his love cannot see her shaky knees and bad hip. He still sees that graceful gait she

33

had when he first noticed it. They have endured lies, possibly cheating, all sorts of disappointments, but yet they remain. Yet they sit on the park bench holding hands and supporting one another. And they know, beyond a doubt, that they are not alone in this world, which makes the world seem less cold and cruel. When you see that old couple look deeply at one another, the whispers that cannot be uttered are saying, "Thank you for giving my life an anchor and saving me from the sting of loneliness through the harshness of living. Thank you for caring, for remaining, for being my reason to keep trying when I failed to try for myself. Thank you for seeing more than I saw in me, for inspiring me to live rather than exist. And above all, thank you for the forgiveness and mercy that kept you loving me when I was not lovable."

Happily ever after for you and I must be worked out and worked at. It isn't easy street. It is the power of will and the honor of keeping the commitment made when things were new and sweet. You know, things don't stay new and too much sweetness is bad on your belly. Life seasons relationships. The key to making it tasteful seasoning is to love hard, ferociously, but never more than you love your Creator and never more than you love yourself. You don't find happiness by forgetting and victimizing yourself for the sake of another. Because how can you truly love your mate if you have not learned love personally by loving yourself? Further, it does not help or empower others to accept abuse. It simply isn't necessary. Truth is, the measure of outer love is self-love.

In my own personal life, I've had way too many failed relationships. Unlike many, I always knew I was the problem. I hadn't been taught how to relate to a man properly. I hadn't seen it except on television. I didn't fully understand how to give love or receive it. Believe it or not, the two cannot be separated. Either you are an open conduit to love or you aren't. And if you aren't, you will not properly accept or give love.

These days, I've learned to love myself and appreciate who I am. I've loved and lost, but the losses taught me so much more than I can explain. Each break up brought lessons. Not all of them were tumultuous, thank God. But all of them were educational. So rather than becoming bitter, I decided to better myself.

In the case of my friend, I watch her live her joy daily. I see the struggles she endures but I see the joy in her eyes when she looks at her husband and it inspires me to keep hope alive, to keep believing that real love is coming. I don't wait silently and aimlessly. I wait as a server waits a table. I wait while reading books, practicing patience, praying myself through the things that could bring pain to my future spouse. I wait without sacrificing my dreams and goals. I wait while working. And I watch the love and joy of others to strengthen me when I feel weak or tired.

If there is anything I want you to get from this book, it is that happily ever after can be yours and should be. You deserve to find a great love, but don't allow your issues to damage it. Work on yourself while you await your king or your queen. Be prepared to serve him or her and love them as passionately as you can imagine and then some. Go crazy in love, doing everything you can to celebrate each other because it is a privilege. In fact, it is God's most blessed gift to the entire world. Nothing tops it! Never have and never will!

Excerpts

Please enjoy the beginnings from *Unnecessary Roughness* and *Heart Strings*.

UNNECESSARY ROUGHNESS
Excerpt

Introduction

Relationships seem to be the primary focus of most people. People want healthy, functioning marriages, families, and friendships. But it seems no matter how hard we try, difficulties occur. People we once shared a meal with become our "enemies" and those we never much cared for become our friends. The person we vow our hearts to sometimes become the person who hurts us the most- on purpose- over, and over again. At the same time, the one we look down upon is the one aching to give us the commitment we're begging others for.

This isn't a tell-all book about who did what and when, though it is factual. But the purpose is not to parade my personal relationship troubles before you. The purpose is to heal those who are, like I was, suffering silently, dying daily trying to cover up the pain in their hearts. I'm only going to ask two things of my readers: read this with an open mind and without judgment. If you do that, I can almost certainly guarantee you won't make as many mistakes. What's more is you'll find yourself free mentally and emotionally.

With that being said, let's get into the meaty stuff. Happy reading!

Heart Strings

Excerpt

Chapter 1

"Many waters cannot quench love, neither can the floods drown it: if a man would give all the substance of his house for love, it would utterly be contemned." Song of Solomon 8:7

Love is a funny little word. As a tenet of my faith, I don't believe love is just an emotion. GOD made Himself equal with love when the Bible said GOD is love. Therefore, in the truest sense of the word, love is a powerful, creative force. It is God. However, for the sake of this book, I want to talk about love from a very limited and human perspective. The way we utilize this term does not even come close to the true power of the word or the entity.

To further prepare you for this journey, let's look at love in its various grammatical forms according to our understanding.

- Love as a verb, an action we take
- Love as a noun, an emotional state
- Love as an adjective, descriptive language of the mind
- Love as an adverb, descriptive language of the heart

In all its various forms, love baffled many because none of those human descriptions can adequately define the entity of Love, the power through which mankind came to be and is kept. But in all the noise of trying to define the force that makes life worth living, there are many underlying truths.

There's not a soul ever created that didn't seek to be loved, according to our understanding of it. We all desire to feel those goosebumps, the flushed skin, the rapid heart rate, the heightened sense of awareness of self, and all the other things that make "love" so addictive. The problem is those things have nothing to do with love, per se. It is romantic attraction and not love that produces those sensations. And so some people go from relationship to relationship trying to hold on to those things and completely lose out on what love truly is.

Love is an entity and action, exists both in the natural and the spiritual, occupies both heart and mind, and exercises power over both flesh and spirit. Some will never understand that sentence because your experiences taint your idea and definition of love. You can't understand the duplicitous nature of love because all it ever was to you was an idea. For others, at the end of this book, you will fully understand what I mean and why I started the first chapter off with such a hard topic to pin down into one book, let alone a simple chapter.

***

My Story

From my earliest memories, I never wanted anything more than I wanted to be loved. I wanted houses, cars, clothes, a husband, children, businesses, money, friends—the list goes on. But right there at the top, never dethroned, was my desire to know for sure that someone loved me. That yearning was both the life and death of many opportunities. Restated, it was my driving force that eventually led me to GOD.

But much before I made it that far, I was from relationship to relationship, friend to friend, place to place searching, even though I didn't know what I was searching for, obviously. I was so empty and unfulfilled that I'd turned into something between a magnet and a leech. Sounds like I'm being hard on myself, right? Wrong! It is in pure honesty that I write these words. I was a huge, gaping black hole sucking the very life out of those in my path because even when I found love, I didn't recognize it or couldn't fully appreciate or reciprocate it.

In my romantic relationships, though each would grow to care about me, it never seemed good enough. After wrestling with me for a few years, they'd find themselves empty because they were trying to fill a hole no one and nothing could fill but the love of God. Yet, they continued to attach their hearts to me, strings and strings of emotional and physical attraction, desire and demand.

In my brokenness, I became entangled and enthralled by each one of them, sucking up all the adoration and affection I could until there was no more. It was addictive, though painful, yet in my addiction to this idealized version of love, I found myself seeking it out elsewhere when the well of demonstrative displays ran dry with each man. Before long, there was a string of broken hearts, bitterness and catastrophe behind me.

While it hurt me to hurt others, I could not for the life of me shake the emptiness that drove me. Even when I wanted to stay, even when I knew I should stay, I could not make my feet stay home or my mind stay attached to what was real and right before me. But with each heart I left broken, I also left a piece of myself. I was probably more fragmented than a used computer with millions of downloads. I had left pieces of myself all over the place. And so I was diluted in strength and character.

With each break up, the next became easier rather than more difficult because I was weaker rather than stronger. Each time I laid down with a man, taking in his essence, I was becoming less of me and more of him. Some people don't believe in multiple personality disorder, and maybe in the traditional, psych definition, I don't either. But what I *know* about is multiple personality disorder from a spiritual sense.

As women, we receive from our men the essence of those men. Done properly, sex is a ministry that continues to mix the two people in blissful ecstasy until they become one. Each time, every moment they are together, they are becoming more and more uniform through their natural and spiritual sexual exchanges. When done wrong, chaos ensues. All those people find themselves fighting for a spot inside each other. Whatever relationship exists is strained, pulled, tugged, pushed, jerked, twisted, bent and chewed until it breaks, most of the time unpleasantly. But just because each of those relationships breaks in the natural doesn't mean they are broken in the spirit.

I knew I had a good heart, a desire to do the right thing and a hatred of all that would cause another person pain. Nevertheless, when it came to my actions, it was as if I could not fulfill my own expectations. In the eyesight of those around me, I was a cruel and unaffected heartbreaker.

That wasn't who I was at all. I was weak, lost, confused, scared and wounded. I didn't want to hurt anyone. I just wanted to be loved. I wanted to share my life and my heart with someone. I wanted to be understood. I wanted a partner in this life I could trust, rely upon and believe in. I wanted someone who would never leave me no matter what atrocities I put them through because somewhere deep inside I knew I had that same staying power and it would take just that much to make me believe. I just wanted someone who could pass all my ridiculous tests.

And much like the tests in the famous line of horror movies, *Saw*, none of the tests could be passed without a huge, inhuman amount of pain. This is the way sexual abuse and parental abandonment can warp you and, man, I was warped and knotted up all over the place. What's more, because the lack of love is what knotted me up, only love could fix it.

I knew I needed love but I didn't know where to find it for a long time so I sought it out in people who claimed to care. But remember, love is bigger, more powerful, and more active than we've grown accustomed to defining it to be. Because I didn't really know what love was yet, I settled for a lot of bad treatment and disrespect in the name of and for the sake of love.

It took some years, but I finally discovered I didn't need man's twisted idea of love. I needed real love, the kind that has curative and redemptive powers. I needed something that was and is rarer than a naturally occurring colored diamond.

Again, this word is often said carelessly without full understanding of what it is or what it can do. If we're easily deceived, we could soon be led to think love is easy to find. It's all over the place verbally, yet it is the most sought after element of life. It always has been. It always will be. We were all created to give love and to be loved. In fact, we were created by GOD (LOVE) in love. So that element is a permanent fixture in creation and ever shall be so.

About The Author

Lacresha N. Hayes is the founder and owner of Lanico Enterprise and Your Healing Partner. She is a publisher at Lanico Media House and Executive Vice President with myEcon, Inc. She is also a trainer and speaker, as well as a social media guru whose estimated online reach is well over 20,000,000 people.

Lacresha has written 30 books and counting with 16 titles currently on the market. She loves poetry and romance and focuses on Christian and spiritual messages.

For more information, or to connect with Lacresha, you can visit her website at www.lacreshahayes.com or connect with her on Facebook at www.facebook.com/lacreshahayes

www.ingramcontent.com/pod-product-compliance
Lightning Source LLC
Chambersburg PA
CBHW071351130626
46556CB00005B/2128